Ankylosaur Attack

To my brothers, James Loxton and Jason Loxton, for all the plastic dinosaur battles we had in our backyard in Metchosin, British Columbia.

ACKNOWLEDGMENTS:
Deepest thanks to Cheryl Hebert, Crystal Cerny, Andre Hebert, Daniel Abraham, Julie Roberts, Sandy Gibson, Pat Linse, David Patton, William Bull, Isaac Loxton, Desiree Schell and K.O. Myers for photographic assistance.

Special thanks to Donald Prothero, Kenneth Carpenter and Jason Loxton for expert paleontological insights. Your generosity is warmly appreciated.

Additional thanks to my colleagues Pat Linse and Michael Shermer at *Skeptic* magazine (www.skeptic.com) for their wisdom, support and ongoing encouragement.

Kids Can Press acknowledges the financial support of the Government of Ontario, through the Ontario Media Development Corporation's Ontario Book Initiative; the Ontario Arts Council; the Canada Council for the Arts; and the Government of Canada, through the BPIDP, for our publishing activity.

Published in Canada by
Kids Can Press Ltd.
25 Dockside Drive
Toronto, ON M5A 0B5

Published in the U.S. by
Kids Can Press Ltd.
2250 Military Road
Tonawanda, NY 14150

www.kidscanpress.com

Edited by Valerie Wyatt
Designed by Julia Naimska

This book is smyth sewn casebound.
Manufactured in Tseung Kwan O, NT Hong Kong, China, in 4/2011
by Paramount Printing Co. Ltd.

CM 11 0 9 8 7 6 5 4 3 2 1

Library and Archives Canada Cataloguing in Publication

Loxton, Daniel, 1975–
      Ankylosaur attack / written by Daniel Loxton ; illustrated by Daniel Loxton with Jim W.W. Smith.

(Tales of prehistoric life)

ISBN 978-1-55453-631-3

1. Ankylosaurus — Juvenile literature. I. Smith, Jim W. W. II. Title.
III. Series: Tales of prehistoric life

QE862.065L69 2011   j567.915   C2011-901280-4

Kids Can Press is a Corus™ Entertainment company

TALES OF PREHISTORIC LIFE

Ankylosaur Attack

Daniel Loxton

Illustrated by Daniel Loxton
with Jim W.W. Smith

Kids Can Press

It was a morning long, long ago — millions of years before humans walked the Earth.

As the first rays of sunlight shone through the trees, a young ankylosaur opened his eyes. He looked around. The cool morning air began to warm up. He turned his huge armored body to bask in the sun.

But wait — what was that new smell? Could it be a meat eater?

No. It was a dinosaur with plates of armor and a club on his tail. It was another ankylosaur!

The other dinosaur was old and big. He had scars from many battles.

The young dinosaur slowly approached the stranger. He knew that ankylosaurs mostly wanted to be left alone.

The old dinosaur was very bad tempered. He had a sore leg. The pain made him want to fight.

As the young dinosaur came near, the old one stomped the ground. He grunted and roared. He waved his tail club back and forth. The message was clear: Go away!

The young dinosaur turned to leave. He did not notice hungry eyes watching from the forest nearby.

Peering through the branches, a fierce meat eater watched carefully. She opened her mouth and showed her giant teeth. She drooled in hunger. She was one of the most dangerous animals in the world — a *Tyrannosaurus rex!*

The tyrannosaur saw that the old ankylosaur was injured. She waited for a chance to attack. She stood quiet and still until ...

Crrraaaaash! The tyrannosaur smashed through the branches. She let out a ferocious RAAAARRRRR! Her teeth glistened. Slobber flew from her enormous mouth.

The old dinosaur turned to defend himself. His tail club was a powerful weapon. If he could swing it fast enough, he could knock the tyrannosaur off her feet.

But it was too late. The meat eater leapt at the old fighter.

The tyrannosaur chomped down on the old one's back. Giant teeth crunched and slipped over his tough plates. She bit down again and again. But her teeth could not cut through the ankylosaur's strong armor.

The tyrannosaur tried something new. She pushed against the old dinosaur to flip him over. If she could get him on the ground, she would bite into his soft belly.

The scarred old ankylosaur had fought many battles in his life. He had survived many dangers. But now he squealed in terror. His sore leg made him no match for a fast-moving tyrannosaur.

His body tilted as she pushed against him. Any second now, he would be on the ground. Any second now, he would be dinner for the hungry meat eater ...

Swoosh! Something heavy swung past the tyrannosaur's head. She jumped back, startled. The old ankylosaur stumbled aside.

The tyrannosaur whirled around and found herself face to face with a new enemy. It was the young ankylosaur!

Swish! Swoosh! The young ankylosaur swung his tail club from side to side. The club whooshed by, just missing the mighty meat eater.

The young dinosaur bellowed at the tyrannosaur and kept his tail ready.

The tyrannosaur roared back. She crouched on her powerful legs. She waited for — now!

The tyrannosaur threw herself at the young dinosaur. But he fought back. He swung his tail as hard as he could. His club whistled through the air.

Thud! The bony club crashed into the tyrannosaur's side.

The tyrannosaur's roar turned into a yelp. She was bleeding and hurt.

She backed away. She could not win this fight. She turned and limped into the trees.

The next day, the young ankylosaur wandered and ate, wandered and ate. He was extra hungry after the fight.

Beside him, the old one ate ferns and bushes, too. Today the old dinosaur did not try to chase the young one off.

Maybe later they would go their own ways. Ankylosaurs were like that. But today, on this sunny morning, they ate peacefully, side by side.